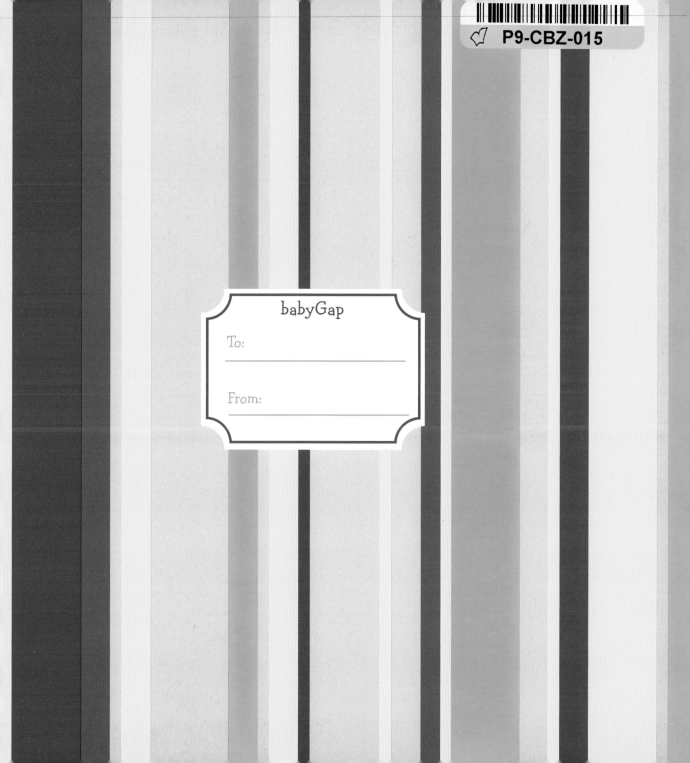

babyGap

To:

From:

Edited by Lisa McGuinness.
Book design by Pamela Geismar.
Typeset in Hank BT.
The illustrations in this book were rendered in acrylics.

ISBN 0-8118-4843-4

Manufactured in the U.S.A.

10 9 8 7 6 5 4 3 2 1

Published exclusively for Gap by
Chronicle Books LLC
85 Second Street
San Francisco, California 94105
www.chroniclebooks.com

Anywhere and Everywhere

By Leslie Jonath

Illustrated by Emilie Chollat

babyGap books

I love you anywhere and everywhere
no matter where we are.
It's so fun when we're together
whether near to home or far.

Let's go on an adventure,
in a car, a bus, or plane.
Then let's ride a tandem bike
and conduct a choo-choo train.

Let's play at the beach.

We'll make castles in the sand.

Let's surf the waves together

and you can hold my hand.

Let's skip to the park
and swing side by side.

Let's climb up the ladder
and shoot right down the slide.

Let's stroll through the market
to pick up apples, eggs, and ham.

CARROTS

Let's not forget the berries
to make sweet purple jam.

Let's go to the zoo
to see the tall giraffe.

Let's surprise the monkey
and try to make him laugh!

Let's join the circus.

We'll flip and twirl and swing.

We'll meet the flying acrobats

and the lions in the ring.

Let's zoom on a rocket ship
and see the shooting stars.

Let's visit the rings of Saturn

then land on planet Mars.

Now let's go back home.
We've laughed and played, it's true.
Anywhere and everywhere,
I love spending time with you.